Abraham O. Hall

The Congressman's Christmas Dream, and the Lobby

Member's Happy New Year

A holiday sketch

Abraham O. Hall

The Congressman's Christmas Dream, and the Lobby Member's Happy New Year
A holiday sketch

ISBN/EAN: 9783337292058

Printed in Europe, USA, Canada, Australia, Japan

Cover: Foto ©Andreas Hilbeck / pixelio.de

More available books at **www.hansebooks.com**

THE

CONGRESSMAN'S CHRISTMAS DREAM,

AND THE

Lobby Member's Happy New Year.

A HOLIDAY SKETCH.

BY A. OAKEY HALL.

ILLUSTRATIONS DESIGNED BY HIS DAUGHTER, CARA D. HALL, AND DRAWN ON WOOD BY
H. L. STEPHENS.

NEW YORK:
SCRIBNER, WELFORD & CO.,
No. 654 BROADWAY.
LONDON:
188 FLEET STREET.
1870-71.

QUOTATORY SYLLABUS.

———— • ◆ • ————

Compiled, at author's request, by Mrs. ALICE EVELYN GOLDSMITH.

———— • ◆ • ————

THE CONGRESSMAN'S

CHRISTMAS DREAM,

AND THE

LOBBY MEMBER'S HAPPY NEW YEAR.

CHAPTER I.

MR. AND MRS. DARBY DILKS were very happy members of the Thespian profession in New York, when the bursting of a cannon converted him into a politician, and transformed her into the keeper of a second-class boarding-house in Washington City.

It was an eccentric decree of fate; but then Darby had insisted upon visiting Washington to witness the inauguration of General Jackson, whom he declared to be the only dramatic statesman in history; and his rashness had driven him to the very mouth of the cannon that, on Capitol Hill, before the ceremonies commenced, belched forth a nation's gratitude.

Consequently, when the cannon burst, Darby suddenly lost an eye and missed the Presidential sight-seeing.

Othello's occupation being gone, the sympathizing Jacksonians made him a Deputy Sergeant-at-Arms in the House of Representatives—a sort of stage-manager over the messengers and pages of that body, to direct their entrances and exits, and their doings both before and behind the flats. A sympathizing administration contributed its patronage—in the shape of department clerks, lobby members, and Washington loungers—to Mrs. Dilks' boarding-house on the Georgetown Road; and when ended the third week of the last December which the Jackson Administration was ever to see, Mr. and Mrs. Darby Dilks had been for eight years on the Jackson stage, performing the parts which fate, as aforesaid, had assigned to them.

The Christmas holidays were coming, and—to use Darby's theatrical announcement at the breakfast-table—Congress was approaching a festival mile-stone, at which the political coach must pull-up for dinner, and shake off the way-side dust.

Darby, on the morning in question, was strutting up and down the rotunda of the Capitol, awaiting the arrival of a brace of pages, who were to be instructed as new appointments, vice Tinsel and Spangles removed for sundry illicit traffickings in members' franks. As he walked, he seemed the apotheosis of the Government—an Atlas carrying the Capitol on his shoulders, sublimely indifferent to the Minerva at the Speaker's desk, or to the Mars at the Opposition benches, or to the Court of Venus in the Senate gallery. He appeared to look around for acknowledgment of his dignity and greatness, notwithstanding the lost Pleiad in his phrenological firmament. Not more did Ulysses

tremble before Polyphemus than did pages before the one eye of Darby Dilks.

The expectant two were dilatory, and the orb rolled impatiently. Presently it glared upon one of them.

The page from long-primer shrank into pearl as the orb became eclipsed with dignified rage.

"How now, sirrah!" exclaimed Darby, in a dramatic blank-verse tone, and with a semi-blank wink of rage. "This commencement bodes nothing auspicious to your future success!"

"If you please, Sir," answered the page, shrinking from pearl into diamond, as the eye seemed to read him over and over and through and through, "it was all along of the Congressman who wanted a package carried to Gadsby's Hotel. He asked was I a page? and I said yes; and he handed me a bundle that had come by mail. 'Public dockyments,' he said; but the paper broke, and them was clean shirts."

"Varlet that you are, why did you not tell him you were not yet sworn into office to support the Constitution, as Darby Dilks understands and construes it—that you were not yet before the scenes! And, page or no page, how dare you pry into honorable members' cheap-home-washing documents!

> Who thus begins to turn his pagèd life,
> Will never play in fortune's pageantry!"

"Naught extenuate, Sir, but listen to my wise counsel; and you, too, Sir," winking the other messenger into the interview.

" Now, just imagine yourself Laertes, each one of you,
and I will be your Polonius—and this is my advice :

> Always be punctual ; and it will follow,
> As the night the day, thou canst not then be late
> To any Congressman.   And don't forget
> Thin shoes that make light noise.   Keep ready eyes,
> Short tongue, long ears.   Blab not without, nor yet
> Within.   Serve all who ask ; and every Saturday night
> Meet me in room No. 8, for stipend money.
> And, above all, remember that you serve
> Your country and General Jackson.

" Now go into the hall and ask for Dutch Mike, the
head page, who will set you to your several tasks."

A portentous shadow here crossed and obliterated the
shadows of the retreating messengers, whose exits were as
sudden as if they had gone through traps in the floor.   It
was the shadow of the Honorable Lysander Lillington,
of Lillington Dale—that terrific M. C., foeman to jobs,
corruption, and the lobby !

" Good-morning, Darby," said the owner of the Shadow ;
" what is the mood of the Administration this morning ?
Does it retrench, or grow extravagant ?   Are we reducing
those useless excrescences of legislation called pages, or are
you adding to the number ?"

And the substance of the shadow gestured toward the
place whence the double-headed Laertes had vanished.

" Merely a substitution—no more, nor less," answered
the Sergeant.   " We leave retrenchment for you Whigs
when you shall get into power.   Those pages belong on
your side of the chamber."

" Small use to me. Do *I* frank even public letters ? Do *I* encumber mail-bags with dirty linen or fraudulent rhetoric ? Who, less than I do, robs the Government of pens, sealing-wax, or knives ? Let the nation answer ! "

The Hon. Lysander addressed himself to a knot of loungers hard by, although he looked at the Sergeant ; and the loungers winked in chorus.

" I am even now on my way to the Library in person, to perform my own page duty."

" Not open yet," replied Darby, with official alacrity.

" Of course not, now I stop to think ! " continued the M. C. " I might have known it. Ten o'clock A. M. is about the hour when the librarians take their Administration cocoa in bed, I presume. Oh, blind nation ! Your downfall approaches ! The days of these States are numbered ! "

Here he gestured as if addressing some imaginary mass meeting in the distance ; but confident of being heard at least by the rotunda loungers and Darby, or perhaps by the stray reporter who was purchasing a sour apple in the corner.

Five hundred M. C.'s in previous years, in the same place, had numbered the days of the republic ; but the days seemed to get on very sunshinily, and in orderly sequence, nevertheless.

So, shaking his head as the five hundred before him had shaken their heads, from the time of the Shay rebellion to the nullification threat, Lysander Lillington, M. C., betook himself to the library of Congress, and inquiring for a duplicate Report of the Secretary of the Treasury, sat down to examine the statistics; mentally resolving soon to move for a Committee of Inquiry into the domestic habits of the Librarian up stairs.

As the hour for the day's session approached, and Darby had gone in pursuit of his appropriate duties, the crowd in the rotunda began to increase. Mingled with the shuffle of feet was a buzz which seemed to confuse into one sound all the conversation of the interlacing groups.

The buzz went up to the dome and down to the pavement again, and then bounding up to the pillars bounced back to the walls, and ran along these in every direction, and out at the porticoes, and down the steps, and through the parks, and up the broad avenues, and circled the Government buildings, and fed the Department offices, and encountering counter buzzes, reduplicated itself on hotel steps and in the bar-rooms, finally to circumvent the President's Mansion, and become a drowned and suicidal buzz in the marshes of the Potomac.

The buzz, or something else, seemed sadly to confuse an old man, who, apart from all the groups, stood before one of Trumbull's revolutionary paintings. It seemed to daze an old dog who crouched at his heels, oblivious of the danger threatened to his tail as it invited the toes of the passers-by in that crushing amusement which belongs to Washington life. His master gazed at the picture in utter unconcern of the crowd, and the dog looked into the face of the old man with that earnestness which belongs to canine appreciation of pat-and-bone kindness.

The veteran was past the Psalmist's verge of life. He leaned upon a stout hickory staff; and as he lifted his

large-brimmed hat from his wrinkled forehead, he showed a few white locks circling a huge scar that appeared to glow and fade in the patriotic sunlight reflected from the battle-scene on the canvas in the panel.

"Courage, Ranger—courage, my old dog; in a few months we will win it," muttered the old man, turning from the artist to the crouching animal.

The dog sprang up from his lethargy in an instant, and with a bark of joyful response leaped toward the picture.

"Hello! you, Sir!" growled a voice from behind a pillar; "we don't allow dogs in here—take it out—take—"

Here the figure of one of the watchmen came forth; but as he saw the old man stretching his staff over the animal protectingly, his tone changed.

"Oh, Captain Sherburne, is it you? You're privileged, you know; but please keep him quiet for 'xample's sake."

"Who is that?" asked a by-stander of the watchman, as the old man and the dog moved on to the next painting —the Surrender at Yorktown—that again fascinated both master and dog.

"Captain Sherburne, Sir; one of the revolutionary heroes; been here these many years, trying to get the Bill for half-pay passed. Spunky old fellow, too. Stuck to the business well. We all know him here. Senator Wright, last spring, took up the Bill, and moved it on. Harry Clay made a speech that brought the gallery crying down-stairs—all about stars, and scars, and battles, and old soldiers. If it gets through the House this winter the old gentleman will have lots of money. Dare say he needs it."

The by-stander, approaching the old hero, took off his hat in salute.

"Sarvant, Sir," said the veteran, and Ranger winked the same thing.

"You are an old soldier, I hear," began the stranger. "I am glad to meet you; for although an English traveller, I honor and venerate the survivors of the old American guard who so gallantly fought for their freedom."

The old man took off his hat in acknowledgment, and the scar disclosed seemed to glow approvingly.

"And I hear, too, that your country neglects you. Pardon me for tendering you a souvenir of my veneration for valor;" and he held out a purse.

Down went the hat over the scar, that shrank into an angry white spot, and "trac" fell the cane with a sharp sound on the pavement. There was a low growl, too, from the dog.

"Englishman! do you dare to insult an old soldier?" said the Captain, again and again "trac"-ing his cane on the floor, while the dog crouched into an ominous heap of mastiff-ship.

"No, sir, my country is tardy—tardy—only tardy—not neglectful!"

The stranger, too astonished or bewildered for immediate utterance, still held the purse in his hand, at which Ranger directed his eyes, as if perceiving in it the cause of offence.

"Has it come to this, that an old soldier is approached in charity by a foreigner, and he a Britisher? Oh, General! General! you wouldn't have thought it." And he turned toward the picture, as if for consolation.

" If language can assure you of the depth of my apology, my dear Sir,—as I see you are offended, and I was indeed abrupt and wrong,—then you may yourself dictate the language."

" That's me yonder !" cried the veteran, not heeding what was said, and pointing with his cane—" that's me to the right of the American column. How young I was— how young—under thirty—and a Captain."

He had forgotten the Present in contemplation of the Past ; which the stranger perceiving, made haste to pocket the purse, and so release himself from the dog's crouch and glare. The Englishman stood as if expecting the soldier to say something more. But the picture and the past were engrossing. So he advanced and extended his hand.

" Sarvant, Sir—sarvant," said the old man, taking it, and now recollecting the matter. " You don't know an old soldier in this land. He asks no charity ; not even from his Government, that must soon do him justice."

So, with a hearty shake of the hand, the intruder on the old soldier's meditations mingled with the groups, and Captain Sherburne, attended by his dog, moved down the east passage toward one of the Committee rooms— Ranger turning about angrily at the picture, as if his master's troubles were some way connected with that.

The room which he sought had printed over the door " Committee on Claims." He knocked at it, and imme-diately a good-humored voice cried " Come in !" and he entered.

" Bow-wow-wow," said a facetious gentleman, at a table

on which were a brace of bottles and a plate of crackers.
" Look here, Smug, here's a bow-wow come for relief."

The facetious gentleman was a youth just installed as
Clerk of the Committee. Smug, (short for Samuel
Smucker, Esquire) had been an old Department Clerk
since the Monroe era of good feeling, and who did the
researches and statistics and speech polishing for the Committee.

" I beg pardon—sarvant, Sir "—began the old man, looking at the young gentleman and his bottles and plate—
" but I see I have made a mistake ; my old eyes deceive
me sometimes ; I thought I saw Committee Room over
the door ;" and he began to bow and to move out.

" Hold on, bow-wow," responded the young man, throw-
ing a bit of cheese playfully toward the dog, who merely
sniffed it and looked up to see if the place was a wigwam
of peace wherein the salt might be acceptably partaken.

" For shame, Bob !" interrupted Smug, now turning
around from his seat at a corner table—" this is old Captain Sherburne and his dog Ranger—one of the Capitol
institutions, Bob !"

" Sarvant, Sir—you have the advantage of me," said the
Captain, advancing, while Ranger, now perceiving in his
master's movements that war was not the order of the day,
snapped down the cheese and came towards the table for
more.

" Samuel Smucker, Esquire, familiarly called Smug"—
responded Bob, doing the honors with a flourish—" Department Clerk and Sub-Committee on Claims, ain't afraid
of any guillotine, although upon its shining blade be

inscribed Marcy's war-cry, 'To the victors belong the spoils.'"

"Hush!" cried Smug, "and cheese the dog, can't you?"

"I want to see the Chairman," continued the Captain, taking a chair.

"Ha, ha, ha! d'ye hear that, Smug?" laughed Bob; "wants to see the Chairman? So do we; don't we, Smug? D'ye see this pile of papers? they want to see him too. Gaze on these four walls; they'd like to see him. But maybe he'll come next year, or the year after."

"Is it about your Indemnity Bill?" said Smug, motioning for silence from Bob. "If so, Captain, Military Affairs has got that."

"Well, you see as how I've been there," answered the veteran, "and the person in charge looked over all the papers and said this Committee had it."

"Maybe it's Pensions, though," said Smug, soliloquizing to himself. "In these days everything gets mixed up."

"It's been in all three through my time" said the old man, somewhat querulously.

"Here, take a drink," cried Bob, recalled to his sense of hospitality by (what he called in confidence to Smug afterward) "the thirsty tone of the hearty old buck." "And it's prime ale—best in the District."

"Thank you. Sarvant, Sir," responded the old man, taking the glass. "Your health, Sir—and yours!"

"And all our healths—bow-wow included," added the facetious clerk of the responsible and attentive Committee.

"And success to the Bill, too," interpolated Smug.

"Been in all three Committees in my time," repeated

the old man, setting down his glass, and wiping the ale-
froth from his lips with a white handkerchief, on which
was written his name, in the neat Italian hand of a lady.

At the sight of it Smug jogged Bob, and said, *sotto voce*,

" Grandfather of the pretty girl who sings at St. Bridget's, that you saw last Sunday."

" At this Bob whistled to himself; and instantly jump-
ing down from the table on which he had been seated, he
advanced to the old man as if he had only then been
introduced, and shook him heartily by the hand, and
next patting the dog in a confused retreat towards the
table.

Remembrances of beauty always confused Bob.   It's a
way those remembrances have with young men who don't
go much among refined and clever women.

" I'm glad you're going to help the Bill," said the old
man, coupling the friendly hand-grasp with his thoughts ;
"and I'm glad it's here, in your keeping."

" But is it?" whispered Bob to Smug.

Smug shook his head, and replied in whisper,

" It's Military Affairs—must be."

The veteran apparently heard the word ; and he repeated,

" It's been in all three in my time ; and I ought to
know something about Committees.   I was dropped from
the Pension-list in 1821, and that brought me first to
Washington, with Lawyer Montrose, who married my
daughter.   He thought he had fixed it : but it proved to
be all a mistake.   I wish he was alive ; but Mary's dead,
too, and now only Agnes left.   Dear Agnes!   The

money's to be for her—and you'll help the Bill—and all three's had it. Then I came again in 1830 to help pass this Bill—"

And here the veteran fell off into incoherent mutterings, taking the glass which Bob had again filled.

"I say, Smug, what is this precious Bill he's talking of? Remember I've just come. Post me, won't you?"

"Oh, a Bill for giving half-pay to the Revolutionary officers. I've heard say that Congress passed such a bill very early in the Government. But before the money was raised another Congress repealed it. Daniel Webster, who's a good friend to the old soldiers, says it's vested rights, and Congress is bound in honor to pass it. The House did vote it once, but it got swamped up-stairs. The old 'un's right; it has been in all the Committees. He's lived here, urging it, for seven years. Wright put it through the Senate last Spring; but the House is getting economical now the Kinderhooker is in."

"Talking of economy," said Bob, a bright idea seeming to strike him, "that reminds me of Lillington—he's on both Committees."

"So he is," answered Smug. "Why, Bob, you're improving! He's minority man on both, because he loves to go in for economy, eh? The Opposition always go in for economy—always!"

And Smug winked with that sagacity of statesmanship supremely felt by all Department clerks of twenty years' service.

"Captain, it has just occurred to us (with emphasis on the word 'us') that the Hon. Lysander Lillington is upon

2

both Claims and Military Affairs, and if you call on him at his rooms you'll find out all about it."

" Sarvant, Sir !" said the soldier, rising from his incoherence as Smug addressed him. " Thank you ; I'll go there to-night."

" Better leave the dog behind," said Bob, opening the door, but thinking of the charming grand-daughter ; " the Hon. Lysander is a wolf-dog on the Treasury-box himself, and very savage, and there might be a fight and trouble, you see."

And so the old man left the sub-Committee to their alternation of public time and private enjoyment neatly adjusted into a Congressional sandwich, the like of which many in Washington bite upon and enjoy under the head of " Stationery."

But the honorable gentleman alluded to deserves, as a veteran member of Congress, a full portraiture. An original Adams man, he had now been eight years in opposition, and was likely to be in the same rank for four years longer. He had a life-lease of his constituency, which, to do him justice, he amply deserved to hold, so long as mental ability and industry demanded. He was however, painfully impressed with his own importance, and held rather extreme notions of economy. Hence his judgment was sometimes warped, and his heart often wronged by his head ; between those two came occasionally a struggle. Born to competency, and having a taste for public life, he had followed politics as a very profession. He had never married—the death of his " sweet-heart," as the gossips of his village said, having left him a true lover through life. But he had adopted the son of a deceased sister, and had educated him to follow in his own footsteps. Ned Leslie, otherwise Edmund Burke Lillington Leslie (the Burke added by the guardian uncle to weigh the Edmund, and mark his destiny with a white stone; and the Lillington joined on by right of adoption : thus making from the alphabet a most respectable tribute to the autograph), had been educated at Harvard (both in the University and the law school), and at the age of twenty-three was living with his kinsman at Washington, carefully adjusting and scaling the ladder of politics.

"He shall be as William Pitt the younger : educated to statesmanship from his cradle," said the honorable uncle, feeling himself, of course, to be every inch Pitt the elder.

But, unfortunately for the political horticulturist, the grapes thus forced refused to ripen ; and Ned, although fond of his law, his poetry, and his literature, and as good a castle-builder as lives under the age of twenty-five, had become thoroughly disgusted with his one year's residence at Washington, and the political connections and society surrounding him. He was loath to let his uncle know it, out of regard to his pride and gratitude for his kindness. At first he was reasonably unhappy. The kinsman's devotion to the duties of place left him much leisure for himself; and while the uncle flattered himself that Ned was journeying from committee-room to committee-room, or cramming in the library, or attending the levees of the great men, or frequenting House and Senate, and so preparing to become the American Pitt, the nephew had

found otherwhere the sweetest solace for his private ambition.

In his rides on the Georgetown Road, Ned had often
noticed with interest the graceful bearing of a young
woman whom he had seen daily entering the Georgetown
school of the Ladies of the Sacred Heart as scholar or
teacher, but he couldn't make up his mind to the exact
relation. A spiteful veil, moreover, had left only to fancy
a tracery of the features.

One particular evening, while on horseback, he saw
some men approach from a lane toward her, and heard a
cry. A few bounds of his thorough-bred, and he was
among them, dismounted, and gallantly beating off the
party, who were of the drunken loungers about Washington.

It is an old story, and one which happens every day
somewhere. But is everything old in heart-stories to be
rejected ? Then let us shut down the windows of Beauty's
conservatories, and keep Cupid out in the cold ; and suffer
his arrows to rust, and the little god to freeze to death,
even in sight of roses and tulips.

The young lady, when her first terror had subsided,
lifting her veil, showed in her features (no need of fancy
now, Master Ned ; and, oh ! how short-sighted that fancy
of yours has been !) such loveliness of gratitude that Ned
then and there carried no heart of his own back to his sad-
dle or to the rooms at Gadsby's, where uncle and nephew
prosecuted together their emulations of Pitt the elder and
Pitt the younger.

Ned felt bound to call the next morning at the humble lodgings to which he had escorted her, as leading his horse, and making that animal a neutral topic of talk. Fate put her hand on the knocker just as the door opened, and she came out for her walk. Must he not do escort-duty so far as the convent door? Must he not talk as he walks? Common politeness demanded all these.

But the Muse of narration construes it far more than common politeness which discovered for Ned, during the hour's walk, that she was named Agnes Montrose, and was an orphan daughter and a teacher in the convent in whose faith her father had, on his dying bed, requested her to be instructed.

She was the grand-daughter of Captain Sherburne. His small pension was barely enough to give him the necessaries of life. But she was as gifted mentally as she had been physically; and her sweet voice and Madonna-like demeanor won for her enough of salary to eke out hand-somely the ways of life for grandfather and herself. And she sang in the Church of St. Bridget's, too; which employ-ment added a trifle more of income. The Sisters would have wished her to live with them; but could she desert the aged relative who was pursuing Congress for that which he knew would give his darling Aggie subsistence and comfort when life, pension, and affection should be left at the cemetery gate?

This, and more than this—unnecessary here to explain—did Ned learn in his repeated visits to the boarding-house of Mrs. Dilks, where lived Captain Sherburne and his grandchild.

The veteran cared not to inquire who Ned was. He

knew him as the benefactor of his child, and that was
enough.   Darby Dilks was proud to have for visitor at
his house the rising nephew and heir of the Congressman;
and he asked no questions and told no tales; though he
often theatrically thought, "Maybe if the Hon. Lysander
knew his Pitt the younger was in love with a pensioner's
grand-daughter, and forsaking the thorny paths of politics
for the roseate lanes of love, he might not be so well
pleased."

This Agnes was an innocent and guileless girl; as igno-
rant of the world's ways as if she had been a dweller in the
Shetland Isles.   She knew only that Ned was good and
kind to her, and had a rich uncle who was equally good
and kind to him, and that she was happy when they were
together, and was missing something when he stayed away,
which is the whole definition of love.

Ned—the sly young Pitt—had read the story of the
lady-slipper which belonged to his prototype and was worshipped so lovingly by him for all his avowed marriage
to his country only, and hugging the resemblance did
not stop to ask whether he was laying up for himself a
large fund of happiness or an incalculable amount of
misery without any medium sum for a margin.

So he concealed his affections and his intimacies from
the uncle, and went on blindly, hoping all would result
well, as many a lover did before him.

The Hon. Lysander might have found the matter out
had he been an early riser, for Ned and Agnes were always
together at the mass.   When her rich soprano voice
trilled from the choir through the sacred edifice, you might

be sure those moistened Protestant eyes down stairs belonged to Ned. But an M. C. in Washington at early-
morning church? Preposterous!

Ned had returned to Washington only the day before
our story begins. He had been detained by home-business
of his uncle, who preceded him by a fortnight. And when
the elder Pitt and the younger parted at the Capitol
gate—the former to hunt up his library statistics and air
his rhetoric with Darby Dilks,—the younger had walked
briskly toward the Georgetown house as truly as the un-
imprisoned needle points toward the north.

While Ned was endeavoring physically to catch up with
his thoughts, that had reached the premises and seated
him in the parlor waiting for her coming and for his tardy
steps, Agnes was preparing for school.

How often those thoughts of Ned had gone up to her
room, picturing it as a temple where saints were on the
walls and angels sculptured overhead, and all the loveliness
of piety hallowing the sacred place!

The temple in question was a small room twelve by nine
—builder's measurement. The carpet was faded, and the
bedstead, chairs and table fashioned of elderly mahogany.
The mantel-piece was wooden, and the doors yearned for
paint. But there was a fairy made one forget all this in
admiration of the fresh lilac wall-paper; or of the frost-
work of curtains, clothing the windows and covering the
bedstead, as in winter the ugly shrub-oak is dotted into
beauty by the newly-fallen snow; or of the dazzling
toilet-cloth, which seemed built up into a wedding-cake
pin-cushion; or of the hyacinths and camellias on the

corner-table, just bursting into flower; or of the cabinet
paintings over the mantel; or of the prie-dieu in the em-
broidered temple behind the bed; or of the parterre of
muslin, silks, and barèges by the half-opened closet-door;
or of the atmosphere of refinement which seemed to be-
lie mahogany and paint and Georgetown Road, whisper-
ing instead of palaces long ago. Was not the fairy that
very one which watches over all women's home-temples, and
blesses this mannish life of ours with recollections and
reminiscences even when we are behind the business desk
or are sculling over the dirty ocean of worldliness?

But the best of things to admire in the temple was the
image in the looking-glass (Ned would have dubbed it
mirror). It showed her in the act of tying bonnet-strings.
The hat, a coquettish black straw, hinting of summer on
outer braids .that were dotted with golden wheat-grains,
but suggestive of winter inside where the quilted lilac silk
rejected the thrifty oil-silk between, and came proudly out
to tinge the cheeks that had no need of tinge when Ned
was by. How would he have loved to stand there, and
with the adoring glance that loverly absence always tem-
pers best, have proceeded to admire the auburn hair—
like flossy silk—and so tender that rimples marked where
the cruel comb had crushed those tender fibres! How he
would have worshipped the blue eyes, which appeared to
him always in the church as saint-light: their niches the
arching brows, and their curtains the 'lashes to be dropped when worship time was over!

But Ned was a square distant when Agnes left the
house, and as the reflection of the mirror stood suddenly at

the corner before him he bounded forward, to seize her hand, as if to repeat the rescue which had led to their friendship.

" Aggie !"

" Ned !"

Not much in those two words as they stand up in clear type—is there? But show me the compositor who can set up the tones which belonged to their utterance at that corner by the Georgetown Road, and, if any such there be, I want to buy his case !

Was that all which was said at the meeting? Was nothing more? Four months gone by, too, since the last one ! I've an idea that if you had seen the lilac come out upon the cheek, in all its pride, from the bonnet, and had heard that sigh from beneath Ned's watch-pocket in the new vest, you would have placed small reliance upon the omission of any of those words like " darlings " and " loves," which can be filched so cheaply and quickly from any dictionary.

First a pause, when the eyes only were speaking ; and then she said,

" Oh, Ned, don't walk with me, please. There, go home —come to-night—I can't."

" Don't walk with you ? Why—why—"

He did walk, however, ten steps or so, and she did also. Her bonnet-strings became loosened, and she twitched them beneath her chin (a mere acorn in shape, with dimples round about for a cup) in that dexterous knot which women manufacture whenever they are flurried.

" Not walk with you, Aggie ? " (The tone was that of a music-box on its last note of a Beethoven waltz.)

" No, Ned, for the Sisters, since the Tennessee elope-ment, have requested that neither day scholar nor teacher should be seen attended on their way to or from school, except by a relative—and *that* you are not, you know, Ned. And I've promised it; but I'm glad to see you. Come to-night. There, good-by. I must keep a promise, and it's for example."

And she hurried on, leaving him in a bewilderment, repeating to himself the words "elopement" and "promise" over and over again, in a tone which, if the Hon. Lysander had heard, would have frightened him from dreams of his own grandeur and the patriotic marriage entertained for his nephew. But how can the best of us keep the diamond Forget-me-not from going off the cushion, out of the win-dow, unless we are by to see or hear the chattering magpie that was watching it from the trees.

II.

It is evening. Congress has adjourned over three days in token of the Christian holiday approaching. The buzz which has been for nine hours fluttering over the city now seeks, moth-like, the brilliant lights of hotel ante-chambers. No part of the buzz, however, has been allowed to enter the suite of rooms occupied by the Hon. Lysander Lilliton and nephew.

That distinguished economist has been writing. His table is loaded down with blue books and red books, calf books and cloth books. Its leaves groan with the weight of figures above it. *Niles's Register* is open on the table at a reference spot. The librarian must have got through his cocoa, by the sight of the books scattered on the chairs around! The shelves of the national book-room had evidently been placed under heavier contribution than the rules allowed.

But the honorable member had arisen, and now stood by the window, addressing the imaginary mass meeting in the distance. There was an unbounded expanse of vacant lots before his vision, ending in marshes; yet his constituency were mentally expanded far beyond the marshes themselves.

He is in the midst of a glowing sentence, as you may see by the majestic wave of his hand, when a knock at the door rouses him.

A servant presents a card.

"Captain Sherburne," he reads.

"And a dog," adds the servant, "with him."

"Leave the dog outside, and show the Captain up," returns the M.C., methodically. "Some party hound, I dare say, after meat, or else some naval captain, with a story of abuses. The Government must come to my doctrine by-and-by. What do we want of an army at all, or of a navy? Wars are over. Commerce is king. Commerce protects itself. Or what need of ambassadors? Trade is the universal diplomat now. It will save the nation millions per year."

The M.C. had turned from the window to walk the floor, as if thus conning a new speech upon retrenchment, when the door again opened, and the old Revolutionary hero of the Rotunda tottered in.

"Take good care of the dog," said he, half turning to the servant. "Don't beat him; he'll lie anywhere if you're good to him: and he's a firm friend."

There were as yet no lights in the room, and the old Captain had not perceived its occupant.

The latter spoke: "Don't trouble yourself about the dog, my good man. I presume our interview can't be long; for my time belongs to my country, who begrudges us any idleness."

"Does it?" said the old man, turning toward the voice and answering sharply. "Does the country begrudge us? —sarvant, Sir."

Candles being brought, the M.C. and the old soldier stood face to face.

"Some beggar," said the former to himself.

"A stern face," said the latter, aside, as both seated themselves by the table, where, besides the other books, an atlas lay open.

"The country is large, and powerful, and wealthy," said the old man, pointing to the maps. "It was otherwise in my prime. I think I loved it more then."

"To what am I indebted for the honor of this visit?" began the M.C., fidgeting uneasily on his chair, as if the guest was an intruder not only upon his twilight reflections, but threatened to also usurp his province of speech-making.

"This," said the old soldier, tapping the scar upon his head as he pulled up the red cap, "and that"—unfolding a printed page, and handing it across the table.

"Hm—m! Senate Bill, 164. Hm—m! I see—the long-talked-of act for reviving the half-pay."

"Introduced upon notice by the Honorable Silas Wright," returned the old man, and borrowing for the nonce the mechanical tone of the clerks.

"And already passed, I see by your memorandum at the foot."

"After remarks by Harry Clay and Tom Benton in its favor—passed unanimously," continued the soldier, in the same tone.

"And now in the House, I see."

"In the House, on reference to a Committee to consider and report," concluded the Captain.

"Well, old gentleman, I perceive you've got the Parliamentary lingo pretty well by heart," returned the Congressman, in a more jocular tone.

" Ought to have by this time. Was here three years in
Jefferson's day establishing my claim to a pension, and two
more years in Monroe's time, after I was dropped—by mistake, they said. It got right after a weary while. And
now this will be the seventh winter I've been here trying
for this bill. It's a good bill, and an honest one, and was
once almost a law, and will make Agnes comfortable when
grandfather's under sod."

The old fellow paused for breath.

" You incorrigible lobbyist !" returned the M.C., breaking
the pause ; " and have you haunted Washington and pestered
members so many years? Who's your member? Why
didn't you correspond with the War Department? What
do you waste your time and money here for? Where's
the report in your favor ? "

These questions were uttered with the volubility and
precision of a martinet Committee-man.

In a saddened tone the soldier made answer : " I have
no member—no home now but here. There were letters
written and sent by the hundred. They were of no use.
No one minds letters in Washington. I've learned *that*
much here. The report in my favor was first made in the
House four years ago ; but it died on the adjournment.
Then I got again on the docket. Last spring I met Mr.
Wright on the cars. He heard my story, and his big
heart opened at once. So did Henry Clay's. They
brought me on the floor. They pointed to my scars. The
bill was passed in an hour."

" There's an example of reckless legislation," cried the
Congressman to the imaginary mass meeting in the dis-

tance, and waving his hand as if to impress the intelligence upon the country. "Benton's great heart, indeed! And Henry Clay's good-nature! What a shameful suppression of parliamentary law and destruction of precedent! No Committee—no report—no stages, and money voted from the Treasury on the impulse of spasmodic patriotism."

The M.C. turned from the mass meeting in the distance to the figure at his table.

"And act speedily, please—time nears—I may not see many Christmases more. I'm ninety years old on New Year's Day."

"Ninety? Hm—m. This looks like imposture," said the honorable member to himself. "These Revolutionary heroes are actually increasing as the time wears on. Here's a chance for cross-examination and exposure. Do you say you are a Revolutionary soldier?"

"*I* don't say so. *This* says so," responded the old man (rubbing his scar), "and these say so" (pointing to his limbs and hair).

"H—m—m—m. Scars are got in street fights, and—"

"You are right, and it *was* got in a street fight," interrupted the old soldier.

"Ha! thought so," and the M.C. turned again for approbation to the mass meeting far away.

"The street fight was at Lexington. I was a boy of eighteen, sent on at midnight from Concord with a message to Adams and Hancock at the Clark House. It was not long after the Pitcairn murder on the green when I was going through the village. 'Walter,' said a man run-

ning by, 'the blood is shed—get a weapon—a scythe—a
gun—an anything.' I had heard the musketry, and knew
what it meant. I still ran on. A scarlet coat on horseback cut at me—me, a boy—an unoffending, unarmed boy,
and here's the scar as the sword glanced by, and I leaped
the fence stunned the moment after, but in that hour made
a man and a soldier." As the old man spoke, the hue of
youth seemed to return and his age to retire.

There was a noise in the entry outside just here, a bark
and a rush, and then a scratch at the door.

"It is Ranger; he must come in; he knows the story all
by heart; he knows I'm telling it; he loves to be by and
hear it;" and, almost straightened back to the Lexington
time, the old Captain opened the door and let in the dog,
who retreated, growling, under the table, near to the chair
of the startled and astonished host.

"I was at Bunker Hill—in the prison ship. I escaped.
I was at Valley Forge."

The door again opened, and ushered in Ned with
another batch of books and papers. The dog smelled
him in an instant, and, bounding at him, began to whine
recognition. Ranger had not forgotten the four months,
any more than his mistress had.

"Hello! Ranger, what brought you here?" said he,
putting down the books; and then, looking around, he
perceived Captain Sherburne. His heart beat violently,
and he would have gone out were it possible.

"You know this dog, then, and perhaps this trouble-
some old soldier here?" interrupted the uncle, rising to
take some of the papers.

" Know the old soldier and his dog? Ay, that he does
—don't you, Ned?" broke in the Captain, "and Agnes,
too?"

" Why, d'ye see," continued the hero, delighted at having found an ally, and turning alternately to the confused
nephew and the wondering uncle, " it was Ned who saved
Agnes from insult last winter. But mayhap you don't
know our Ned?"

" I should think I ought to, Sir," returned the M.C.; "he
is my nephew and adopted son."

" Then he has told you all about it," the hero eagerly
continued. " Why, Ned, you never spoke to us down at
Darby Dilks's that you were nephew to a Congressman,
and my bill so important."

" Will you explain this rigmarole, Sir?" said the Hon.
Lysander, employing his most oratorical tone, and using
his severest parliamentary manner to his nephew, whom
Ranger still persecuted with embarrassing attentions in the
corner by the door.

" There, Captain!—good-night to you. I'll try and help
the matter," began Ned, somewhat recovering himself, and
anxious for the departure of the old soldier—opening the
door for him, and whistling off Ranger.

" Thank you, Ned—thank you;" and the young man
soon led him to the front steps, and, retracing his way
again, met his uncle.

Ned's story was short, and to the point. The era of
veracity, long dreaded, had dawned. He told the truth,
the whole truth, and nothing but the truth, to his astounded
and enraged uncle, who stormed and swore alternately at

Darby Dilks's lodging-houses, his nephew, and the old man and his girl (as he termed her harshly to his nephew's burning ears), not forgetting the dog—in dread of whom, the legs trembled as he paced to and fro. He recapitulated his benefits to his nephew, and adverted to his hopes and his plans. How had care been rewarded with hypocrisy and concealment! How was the future imperilled with this foolish fancy of a girl in a third-class Washington lodging-house! Was not Ned to wed his country? Or, if he married, was it not to be for power, and family, and influence? Did he love the person? Had he asked her in marriage? Had he written to her? How far was he compromised? These and other questions came at Ned like a *feu de joie.*

" No, I have never said a word to her on the subject. We love—and that is all."

"Oh! that is all, Mr. Romeo, is it? We love—do we? Promise me, Sir, by all that you regard in the memory of your mother, who placed you under my charge on her dying bed, that you will not see her again."

While the uncle was enraged and stormed Ned seemed to recover all his energies, and became cool, silent, and thoughtful. In a low, sweet voice he said, " Uncle, were *you* never in love?"

The veteran politician dropped on the nearest chair. Loosing his cravat, he motioned to the door of Ned's bedroom and study. And without waiting for an answer to his demand, the M.C., quivering either with rage or a new emotion, sought his own.

" Poor Agnes ! you will expect me," said Ned to him-self, " and I cannot come."

She did expect him, and waited for him in her little room until the Captain returned to tell her " it was all right now. He had found out that 'our Ned' was the son of a rich Congressman who had their bill in charge."

Agnes waited, and her heart told her all was *not* right now ; that something had happened. But, retiring to her little oratory, she forgot her new-born fears in accustomed prayers.

Nor were her eyes the only ones which looked upon a Madonna picture that night before the solemn bed-time. The so recently worldly-minded and angry M. C. stood beside his cabinet with a miniature before him. As he gazed, he seemed to read, written upon the forehead, " Uncle, have *you* never loved ?" and to hear the words spoken over and over again by the lips of the portrait. He thus looked and so heard that night, long after Ned and Agnes, in their respective dwellings, were sleeping the hopeful sleep of youth ; and long after the old soldier had commenced, under leadership of the god of dreams, to fight over the past, with Ranger crooning in his doze before the fire, and to look toward a speedy fulfilment of all his holy wishes for his grand-daughter's competency in life.

III.

BUT however great had been the victory of the heart during his midnight vigil over the head, the latter resumed its sway when, on the next morning, the Congressman entered the Capitol grounds, and came within that atmosphere which to breathe seems to transmute all emotions into the one controlling passion of ambition; so that even deputy clerks hope to become Presidents or Cabinet ministers.

Again encountering Darby Dilks in the rotunda, Mr. Lillington took him severely to task for aiding and abetting his nephew in a love intrigue with the offspring of a mere Capitol hanger-on—a beggar for national charity and, mayhap, an old lobby impostor, whom the present generation might be credulous enough to support.

"My worthy Sir," said Dilks, in his dramatic style, but keeping to the political rôle, " *my* policy is masterly inactivity in everything not directly concerning *me*. The young lady is beautiful and accomplished, although a portionless teacher. The young gentleman, for aught I knew, was his own master. How could I check the course of love, or interrupt its seeming smoothness, with any impertinent pebbles?"

And when Darby came home to dinner he imparted the interview to his bustling wife; who, making haste to Agnes's room after dessert, proceeded to a well-intentioned but mortifying conversation.

The holiday vacation in the convent school had that day commenced. Agnes had whispered the night before to herself, " He will hear of this vacation to-morrow morning, and will come to see me then."

Instead of Ned came Mistress Dilks, whose ideas of crossed-love affairs smacked of the Nurse scenes with Juliet that she had been accustomed to play in upon the stage. Agnes, after the womanly aggravator had retired, sought her grandfather, and from him learned how Ned had been cross-examined by the uncle, and thus brought to the old man's comprehension the truths ruthlessly impaled by the tongue of Mrs. Dilks.

" Dost thou love him, Aggie?" said the old man. Clasping his neck, she sobbed upon his shoulder an answer which stretched his age-worn heart-strings to an agonized tension.

Meanwhile Ned commenced to tutor himself into obedience to his uncle, unto whom he felt he owed education, and intellectual nurture, and gratitude of no common grade. But the hours lagged heavily by during two days of separation that succeeded so brief an interview, and one so liable to cruel interpretation. The third was Christmas Day, which, on this year, came with Sunday.

He now knew where to see her. Impliedly he had promised not to visit or to write to her. Perhaps absence, without explanations, were best. No trysting had been consecrated as yet. But to meet her going to church, or returning thence, would not break his resolutions, nor cross his uncle's request.

There is no casuist like the lover.

Awakened early on the Christmas morning, Ned walked, fasting, to St. Bridget's, and again listened to the dear voice from the hidden choir, swelling and dying away through the edifice. He fancied that it was sweeter than ever—as if, losing some of earthly tones, it sought for higher sympathy.

Contrary to the custom of almost a lifetime, the uncle had also arisen early on Christmas morning; still, all of the second and third nights the portrait came between his eyelids and that world of sleep into which his vision sought in vain an entrance, and during all these second and third nights the question, " Uncle, have *you* never loved?" seemed whispered into his ears. Mingling with a little crowd of church-goers, and swayed by irresistible impulse, he found himself in the church. That voice from the choir! This well-remembered voice! Those tones which carried him back many, many years! Were they delusions, or did the dead speak and sing to his mortal ear? Thus questioning himself, the uncle at the church-gates encountered his nephew, when service was over—each surprised, but each repressing its manifestation.

" Ned," said the former, with more of kindness in his voice than he had used in two days, "have you ever been here before ?"

The start was equivalent to an affirmative; and so the elder accepted it, as he continued :—

" But who is the singer ?   Is that the attraction ?"

" It is she—the old man's granddaughter," was his simple and touching answer, as his voice somewhat broke.

"Am I ever to be thus tricked into feeling, and conquered into a foolishness?" cried head to heart. His uncle turned the corner, saying to Ned,

" Meet me in an hour, at breakfast."

"Alas! I shall not see her, after all," he said ; "for he has turned to the side street into which she will enter, and I dare not follow."

So, with heavy heart, he walked toward his room.

As Ned anticipated, the parties met by the choir-door. The soldier recognized the Congressman, and, taking off his hat, said,

" Sarvant, Sir! and a merry Christmas to you! But remember the old soldier. Don't forget Lexington and the prison-ship, Sir; and that I'm ninety years old on New-Year's Day."

Instinctively the proud politician had paused and raised his hat, as Agnes threw back her veil and sadly smiled. The old man had whispered to her,

"'Tis Ned's uncle, my dear!"

More illusion? Was this the face of the miniature? No! for the original of that had been food for worms many Christmases ago. Yes, it was illusion. Some trick here. Grandfather and nephew were leagued together to lead head away, and give the heart the mastery. Sherburne! He had never known one of that name. Not one of *her* family had been—yes, one. And he? Why, he was dead, too—unmarried. Ay, it was logically a delusion, and an illusive snare!

Thus he thought and pondered, as he walked hastily and moodily away, leaving his abrupt courtesy to Agnes's sorrowing remembrance ; for not even Ned was with him.

Nor during the breakfast meal did he exchange a word with his nephew, beyond commonplaces of the usual stamp when conversation, like appetite, becomes forced.

He had been invited out to a Christmas dinner, as had been Ned. The latter pleaded sickness, which the uncle understood. The Congressman went, however, and proved himself the merriest of the party—head before heart this heat! The atmosphere was congenial. The Cabinet, the diplomatic corps, army and navy, and the beauty of the Capitol, each sent representatives to the perfection of the feast. And as the repartee chased the bottle round, and good fellowship awakened old resolves of family pride, the Hon. Lysander Lillington forgot the portrait and the delusion, and wondered how long it would be before Ned should drop his fancy, and, dismissing the pensioner's daughter, who taught in a convent school upon week-days, and sang every Sunday in a Catholic church, choose a wife —if wife he must have, to distract ambition—from among such representatives of birth and family fortune as were now up-stairs in the drawing-room, enjoying the merry Christmas in a properly dignified way.

But at eventide, in the solitude of his own room, the Congressman remembered the choir voice and the face by the church door, and the merry Christmas greeting from the old hero, who bade him think of Lexington and the prison-ship, of suffering and of victory.

And so remembering, with the counter exhilaration of the feast withdrawn, their faces and voices seemed strangely to mingle. Next, shadows of the olden time passed before him and gathered about his arm-chair. The portrait arose

out of its case, and, assuming the robes and mien of the
Goddess of Liberty, came between the table and the
Christmas log in the fire-place, and seemed to motion him
into dreamy silence. Delicious music lulled his senses, as
the figure, radiant with the beauty of maidenhood, pointed
upward. There were sweet hymns which he heard; and
their burden was of martyr faith and martyr triumphs in
the holy cause of liberty. As the music would for a time
cease, the goddess would wave her cap toward the familiar
Capitol, as seen from his window. It would seem to van-
ish, and in its place would appear scenes of the by-gone
Revolutionary time.

"Hearken, the earliest martyr anthem," said the maiden
in the panoply of liberty, still stretching her beautiful hand,
crowned with the starry cap, toward him. And immediately the invisible choir, with the one remembered voice
sweetly predominant, sang: "How great for our country
to die, in the front rank to perish; firm with breast to the
foe, victory's shout in the ear, long they our statues shall
crown and in songs our memory cherish; we shall look
forth from our heaven, pleased the sweet music to hear."

The anthem died away, and eye taking the place of ear
in the dreaming man, he saw stretching before him, as
though he stood upon an eminence, miles and miles of a
New England landscape, a city in the far distance, surrounded by hills on three sides, and the ocean encompass-
ing it on the fourth. Sounds of fife and drum in all its
streets, and scarlet uniforms gleaming in the setting sun.
Troops forming into column. Guards and pickets standing at all the streets and roads of egress. None but uni-

forms permitted to walk or ride away from the city. But as
the serried column march rapidly along one or two figures
are more hastily stealing in advance, crouching under stone
walls, and in the angles of the roads, or cross-cutting fields
and skirting the woods—sometimes entering houses; always with finger on the lips and pointing backward, as if
to say, "They come; patriots, be ready!" The sun de-
clines, and twilight precedes the night; and yet under the
sentinel stars the troops march and the scouts precede.
Candles burn all night in houses on the route, and lanterns
warningly swing from upper crevices of church steeples.
Miles away from the city of scarlet uniforms, that is now
in deep repose, men are hastily moving in all the villages,
wheeling cannon into thickets, and burying casks and bags
and leaden bullets under ground, or beneath barn floors.
Midnight passes; the bells toll two; upon a village green,
before a rude, square church, resolute men, old and young,
in yeoman dress, with various fire-arms, are drawn up in
hasty semblance of military rank. The stars fade away
into the dawn. The morning comes cold and raw. From
the road toward the city is heard by the meeting-house
array the sound of drum and fife; and soon the scarlet
uniforms, that have been marching all the night, stand
before the yeomanry. "Disperse, ye villains! Disperse,
ye rebels!" cries the man on horseback, drawing sword
and wheeling from the sanctuary of peace to fulfil the
butchery of war. Fast to the ground stand the yeomanry.
The insult is repeated, and for home and for family and for
native land they level the private fire-arms, as the serried
guns of an oppressing nation meet them muzzle to muzzle.

Flashes, and sharp reports, and then the dull clouds overhead scud more grayly as the smoke arises; and next the dewy sod grows more dank as life-blood is poured upon the village green. The yeomanry disperse to cornfields and hedges; and scarlet uniforms vaunt themselves before the church door as the sunlight comes to drive the clouds away, and to smile upon the scattered yeomanry who rally and make further stands for liberty in villages beyond. Not far from the scene of massacre a beardless boy has been escaping over a stone wall, when toward him gallops scarlet uniform on foaming horse; there is an uplifted hand, a flashing sword, and the boy falls, turning face upward, and the features present the young impression of the hero's face who had led this young maiden, now in the guise of a goddess, into the Christmas choir at St. Bridget's. But list again; a strain of the anthem arises: "We shall look forth from our heaven, pleased the sweet music to hear; we were firm with our breast to the foe and victory's shout in our ear."

"Gaze once more," whispered the sweet voice of the liberty maiden to the Congressman, dreaming in his Christmas chair.

He sees a valley scooped out from bold and rugged mountains, surrounded with ruined mills and deserted forges. He beholds eleven thousand men in Continental array defile around the mountains, and deploying throughout the valley—for days they come, and for hours they march to and fro. The eastern horizon is heavy with snowbanks, and the winds from the mountain tops sweep down cuttingly to the marrow, and still the blood-current. The sound of axes echoes through the woods. Trees fall. Rude huts arise—slab-roofed and plastered with clay. Coatless veterans and shoeless recruits walk to and fro; some with fagots on the back, and others harnessed to artillery cannon-carriages, upon which the heavy timber has usurped the place of cannon. Now the snow falls in driving fury, and the rude huts that have thickly arisen in the valley and over the mountain gorges are weakened with the drifted weight upon them. Blanketless and breadless, with the coarsest food, to be cooked over scanty fires, the eleven thousand crouch by day and night in the snow-crowned huts amidst the desolation of winter, and await with holy hopes and brave hearts the dawning of some brighter era. "Hunger and nakedness howled like wolves throughout this camp at Valley Forge. There destitution held her court, and ruled with icy sceptre." Such came the burden of another anthem to the dreamer's ears from the invisible choir.

"Look closer yonder," said the sweet voice, directing her cap-crowned hand into a depth of the forest. Lying upon straw, on the outermost hut of all, was the same young man who had been cut down at the fence-side by the sword of the scarlet uniform. Scurvy in his eyes and in his blood and in his limbs, and scurvy binding the young patriot to an inert bed, with scarce a blanket above him. His lips move. Draw near. Are they curses at his lot? Bend the ears closer down.

"Bear on, stout heart! My Concord home was sweet; but suffering for liberty is sweeter still. The red-coats killed my father; and though this be night, joy cometh with the morning."

" Behold yet one more scene," said the liberty maiden.

In a copse carpeted with snow and hung about with frost-ed fringes, and by the side of a frozen creek, there kneels upon the crunching ice a patriot General. His arms, put forth from beneath a gray mantle, are folded across his breast ; the tears are rolling down his cheeks ; and the winter wind hushes itself to deep silence as rises, amidst the cheerless scene, a fervent prayer for courage and re-lief. As the dreamer gazes the invisible choir sings, and over all the sweet voice of St. Bridget's service : " Oh, who shall know the might of the words he uttered there : the fate of nations turned by the fervor of a prayer ! And wouldst thou know the name of the wanderer thus alone ? Go read, enrolled in heaven, that prayer of Washington."

The dreamer, tightening his hands upon his chair, seemed wrestling with some potent spell. His breast heaved, and the tears streamed from his closed eyes. But still, with his mental vision, he saw the sweet figure pointing down that vista of the Past.

And he beholds the hulk of a dismantled ship, anchored upon the bosom of a peaceful bay, near to a smiling village. Toward the southward, into the embrace of ocean, a broad harbor. Before the mocking figure-head of horns of plenty, pouring forth fruits and flowers arise the forest hills of a future metropolis. At the stump of a mast flaunts the red cross of St. George.

But smiling village, and broad silvery harbor, and horns of plenty, and quiet forest hills, are around only to mock the thousand wretches who call this dismantled ship at once their home and catacomb. Toward it a boat steers its way, crowded with patriot forms. How resolute, how noble, how stalwart they look! Resoluteness—alas!—to wane amidst foul air. Nobleness—alas!—too soon to weaken before the filth of a prison-ship. And stalwart forms—alas!—to shrink into skeletons with unwholesome food, tortured by thirst, suffering for the nursing of the far-away home, and only despair and contagion as the handmaidens of the crowded hatchway. See! from the boat cheerfully leaps up, as if to defy the oppressor's gaze, the form of the young soldier yet outlined in the wearied frame of the Hero of the Rotunda and the suppliant for a nation's charity.

They register his name in a huge book—a catalogue of funeral gloom. They march him over the deck, and thrust him down a hold.

How the defiant gaze of upper air has been already deadened at the sight of the hundreds upon hundreds here covered with filthy rags; unshaven, unwashed men, with vermin unheeded creeping over their half-naked limbs! The sunlight pours mockingly down, and the aggravating sounds of liberty are heard from shore to shore. Night comes. Face to back the hundreds upon hundreds lie down to sleep, turning from right to left upon the universal oaken bed at the derisive word of command from the midnight sentinel.

Morning dawns, and down the steaming hatchway is heard the never-varying and daily-spoken voice: " Rebels, turn out your dead ! " Every week they muster the dying prisoners on the deck, and at the capstan stands the King's sergeant: " The bounty and liberty for enlistment in the royal service, if you will. Captivity and death is the refusal."

But weekly ever in vain; the King's sergeant turns away, and his bounty-money rusts in the pocket of his flaunting uniform amidst the patriot rags.

" List to the final martyr-hymn," whispered the sweet voice; and the choir sang in the dreamer's ear in touching strain :—

" By feeble hands their shallow graves were made : no stone memorial o'er their corpses laid : in barren sands and far from home they lie : no friend to shed a tear when passing by."

And then, as the music died finally away, the figure vanished, and the scenes closed, and the chimes of midnight ended the Christmas Day.

But still the Congressman sat, with the greeting of the soldier uppermost in his mind, and could not shake the fancies off.

Would he not now remember Lexington and the stricken youth, the prison-ship and the hero whom suffering could not bribe nor starvation win from the patriot conflict ?

Would he yet kindly answer his nephew's question : " Uncle, have *you* ever loved?"

IV.

NEXT morning after Christmas Day Captain Sherburne was unable to rise from bed. It was evident he had caught a severe cold—perhaps from standing in the transept of the church in the early morning, waiting for Agnes. She had been often during the night into his room, and at times had found him in a severe fever and flighty—muttering now about the Bill, and then of Ned, and next as if deprecating the Congressman's anger, and again repeating over and over the battle scenes of the past, or childishly importuning his grandchild for a song—Ranger keeping incessant sentinelship beside the fire, and looking wistfully into her eyes each time her footstep stole softly in.

She hastily determined to seek a physician ; and having been promised a speedy call from an army surgeon near by, who had always been kind to the old man, she returned to his bedside.

"I fear for the result at his time of life, my dear Miss Montrose," said the medical gentleman, "unless his mind can be composed. It is evident that if even false hopes could be excited for the project so near to his heart, that their cherishing would immediately relieve him ; and you must do your best."

"Why not try the truth?" said Agnes to herself when the surgeon had retired, leaving some opiates in the room. "Why not seek the Congressman himself, and if he be angry at grandfather and at me for Ned's account, say to him that which may appease him, even though it bring me sadness and desolation?"

That same love which, in a few days, had shown to her more of her heart than she had ever understood before, now taught her both policy and tact.

"I will go instantly," said she. And stopping for a moment in the lodging-house hall below, to consult the inevitable Congressional directory to be found in all places at Washington, she was soon at the door of the uncle's rooms.

He was home, and alone; for there remained yet one Congressional vacation day. And as he sat in the chair of his dream, with the untasted breakfast before him, it was apparent that in the struggle of heart over head the former had made most headway; particularly as Ned had that morning suggested that he should now be permitted to quit Washington and return to his legal pursuits, as the readiest method of breaking off the intimacy that his uncle repudiated; coupling the suggestion with the request to be permitted a parting interview for explanation.

This head-and-heart wrestle was at its height when the servant announced a young lady, and Agnes entered.

With perfect self-possession she advanced to his greeting ; for at the first he did not recognize her, until, lifting the veil, again he saw the face of the portrait! Misconstruing his agitation and emotion for anger, she proceeded at once to the object of her visit.

" I believe I address the Hon. Mr. Lillington?"

He bowed without speaking, and as the voice filled his

ears he substituted a large easy-chair for the less comfortable one she was about taking.

"And *I* am the granddaughter of that Captain Sherburne who called upon you some evenings since in reference to his Bill. I greatly fear that some misapprehension has come from the old gentleman's absorption in his scheme of life—one which is part of his soul, as schemes so often become when brooded over, whether ambitious or otherwise—"

—Her auditor winced somewhat here, as heart whispered to head that this was true, too true,

"—And that the misapprehension may warp your feelings toward him. Did he speak of Mr. Edward, your—your—"

At this point of the communication, begun with so much self-possession, her voice faltered. Clearly in this atmosphere of the room heart was fast conquering head on all sides! Especially clear was it when the Congressman, in a softened voice, interrupted:

"Pray do not be agitated, Miss Sherburne."

She recovered herself, and added: "If you please, Sir, that was my mother's name. I am the Captain's granddaughter. *My* name is Montrose."

"Montrose!" ejaculated Mr. Lillington, rising suddenly to his feet; "and your father's name was Montrose!"

She also had arisen, and the full light shone upon her face. Her bonnet had fallen back, and the auburn hair rippled in the sunbeam, while the Madonna features paled with inward agony.

"Yes, Sir—Alexander Montrose."

" Merciful Powers ! it is *not* delusion, and the dead *do* speak !" he exclaimed with energy, sinking upon the chair, while she moved toward the bell-rope.

" It is nothing ; do—do—not ring," he gasped ; "at least not yet. And your father ?"

" Immediately upon the death of a beloved sister he went into another part of the country from that in which he was bred."

" Ah ! *my* Nelly—my Nelly !" gasped the proud man to himself.

She was standing now by his side, and her presence overpowered and yet soothed him.

" Your father," he continued, taking her hand most tenderly, " was my college friend. I was to have married his sister. I—I—but why speak of it ? I alone was to blame. It was all my accursed pride and anger that did it. But she died long ago. And I suppose your father never mentioned her nor me."

" My father died when I was yet a child, and so did my mother," she added, this time placing both hands in his, so glad in her joy ; and with the tact and adroitness subdued by the girlish tenderness of her nature, for she had found a father's friend in Ned's kinsman, and all—all must be right.

All was right. How should it be otherwise ? He brought the portrait from its case, and showed her aunt to her in all her virgin loveliness.

" So much like you," he whispered to her, as she bent blushingly over the ivory. " I heard her voice in yours, yestermorn, and thought it delusion."

He told her—he, the proud man of last week to the

young fondling of to-day—of his past, and of his quarrel with the love of his youth. And then they talked of the grandfather and of his pet scheme. And she spoke of his midnight mutterings and wish for songs, while he, surprised at the coincidence, narrated the dream, and how he heard the patriot hymns. And next they spoke of Ned. But here she became silent and arose to go.

"Don't think to escape him; for he shall be there, even at the house of despised Darby Dilks," he concluded, smilingly, as he kissed her hand at the door.

Beat away, hearts! Throb away, with vein and artery in mill-race play! Be calm and tranquil, statesman head! The victory is with youth and hope and love and memories of the past; for policy and pride are by the wall, fast bound.

So he called her back from the stairs, and, whisperingly, said: "I shall not see you again until New-Year's Day— the old man's birthday. I will call to take you to the morning church. It is Sunday, you know. Ned and I will both be there, and perhaps we shall have for his New-Year's dinner a birthday present that will make him young again."

Again he kissed her hand, and waved her smiling on her way.

She thought she breathed an amber atmosphere, and trod upon rose-leaves on her way to the old hero's bedside —so happily she breathed and lightly walked in the crisp December air.

Crumpling bonnet and dress as she fell on her knees by her grandfather's pillow, her auburn ripples flowed over the scar and clothed it with youth, and her lips touched the

wrinkles of age into smoothness, as she then and there whispered it would all go right, and how she had seen Ned's uncle, and that he must not fret again, because, in the holy ways of Providence, whose praises all, whether with voice or heart, had sung that Christmas morning, the difficulties had proved to be but preparations to success, and angels in disguise.

V.

ANÒTHER next morning, when a thin House of Representatives meets for a day or two of tussle with public
affairs before the nation again goes to the wall for a New-
Year's day or two of private rest and enjoyment.   As the
Speaker glances at the clock and strikes his gavel the
Chaplain offers up a fervent prayer, that goes wandering,
spiritless, through the empty galleries and around the vacant desks.   Some of the M. C.'s are at their homes eking
out the vacation, and spending in holiday fun the per diem
pay that the clerks down here are scoring up.   Others are
at the late and stereotype Congressional breakfast, made
up of a digestive alternation of manuscript and eggs, beef-
steak and *Globe* or *Intelligencer* newspaper, cold public
documents and hot coffee.   A few are lounging in the
corridors, extending graciously the Congressional button-
hole to the constituency finger.   Darby Dilks is chasing
up the pages in the lobbies, who are comparing notes on
Christmas-boxes.   And while the Journal clerk begins to
chant the manuscript *pot pourri* of the last day's proceed-
ings, the members, one by one, appear, and the galleries
gradually fill up from the *coteries* of lobbyists and curiosity-
mongers, to whose service the fat deputy-sergeant at the
narrow stair-head is so pie-crustedly devoted.

While the clerk chants, the minute-hand of the clock

goes sulkily around, until chant and tick seem together to say, "This is all a Buncombe business at best, and 'twere better for the country were it put to rest. Politics is but a horse-race after all, and when the winner's put into his stall, up the turf springs green again; while the booth and stands remain until comes next racing-day, and the crowds go dustily away to cure shouts, oaths, and bets freely spent upon their pets. One nag is vicious, and another something moral, as one horse is bay and the winning mare is sorrel. One colt is Southern thoroughbred, and another Western fed; but they all come together when the sweepstakes are put up, and the spoils and jockey-hunters see the shimmer of the cup. In this Congress-stud of ours there is many a fast-time nag, our Inevitable Destiny, for instance, that we brag. One Pegasus to dash away, despite constituency-curb, another that's a galled jade that editors disturb. Uncle Sam's a first-rate groom when his curry-comb is siller, and the feed he gives his horses is the choicest from the miller; but do the sweepstakes, after all, enrich the States, both great and small?"

Thus the chant and the click were in the midst of their roundelay, and the buzz of the rotunda was getting on its full head of steam, when the Hon. Lysander Lillington was busily engaged in consulting fellow-committeemen. And when the Journal clerk drowsed to his desk, and the day's business began in earnest, that economical M. C., to the surprise of the whole House (and each man so surprised that he forgot to object), asked unanimous consent to make a report.

He proceeded to read, from hastily-adjusted manuscript,

that, while at Valley Forge, General Washington had
urged upon Congress provision, by half-pay during life, for
the officers of the army; and that Congress, by a small ma-
jority, had at first sanctioned it, and subsequently recon-
sidered it; and that from the first administration of one
General to the last administration of the present General,
the question had been left open, while the survivors were
rapidly dying, and justice was tardy.

The buzz had flown into the lobbies as he rose to read,
and was now flitting about the floor, hither and thither,
everywhere. What miracle was this? He who was the
universal objector—the mill-dam of all legislation—the op-
ponent of every scheme on the Treasury—and a man in
Opposition, receiving unanimous consent to make a report
in favor of the Bill to award half-pay to Revolutionary officers; and a Bill so young as to have only been kept in a
committee-room over recess, when all parliamentary usage
demanded it should become hoarse with bawling in the
lobby for admission!

And so, amidst the buzz and the astonishment, no resolute objector arose to pay off the Hon. Member in his own
coin; but the Bill of the old hero was now on the House
docket, ready for action upon it in Committee of the
Whole, to the next one of which, still by the consent of
buzz and assent of the miracle-astonished House, the Hon.
Committeeman forthwith moved it, and found it accomplished.

The ensuing Committee of the Whole would be upon
the next day but one, and before it arrived he would
recount the old man's history to the members all about,

and deify him in their eyes, even as the Christmas dream
had showed him worthy of the task.

The invalid Captain rapidly revived when the promise
to his ear by the granddaughter was realized to his
dimmed eyes by the sight of Agnes and Ned again
together, and likely so to be through life. Darby Dilks
had his own ideas of what was up ; but, in pursuance of
his policy of masterly inactivity, made no interference, and
said nothing except to his wife, which being in confidence,
must not be repeated. Smug and clerkly Bob, in the
Committee room, grew jocose over their bottle, drinking
the health of the "glorious old file of a revolutionary
hero" that had come it so 'cutely over the stern-faced and
hard-policied Lysander Lillington, of Lillingtondale, M. C.,
etc., etc.

Nor was that honorable gentleman's head or heart idle
during the two days rapidly passing. His horse had stood
for a full hour before the Georgetown Convent, and his
frank had been upon a letter addressed to his Grace, the
Right Reverend Catholic Bishop of the diocese. He had
entertained many of his adherents and some of his enemies
at an impromptu dinner-party. But he had nevertheless
kept away from Captain Sherburne, and once denied himself as he and the dog left card and bow-wow at the door,
and had been taciturn to Ned ; only saying, " Bring Miss
Montrose (how he loved to say the name aloud to Ned,
and privately to himself, in the seclusion of the library !),
her grandsire, and yourself to the House gallery on Friday,
and let us see whether the day will be unlucky or no."

Friday arrives ; and so does the Speaker at his desk,

and the chanting Journal clerk below, and so in due time comes the Order of the Day, after much rigmarole of Mr. Speaker, and hurrying up and down the aisles of pages with little bits of paper in their hands, as if they were political doves with olive-branches during deluge-time.

"The House is now in Committee of the Whole on Senate Bill No. 164, entitled, 'An Act to provide for the establishment of a back half-pay fund for officers in the Revolutionary War, and for other purposes,'" says a portly member who is called to the chair by the retiring Speaker, according to the etiquette of the occasion. The clerk chants the same announcement. And the reading of the Bill being dispensed with, its title is a third time announced; when, surrounded by the buzz, and faced by Ned and Agnes and the old soldier in the gallery, the Congressman arises to move that the Committee rise and recommend the passage of the Bill. But before perfecting his motion, he proceeds, with a fervor of eloquence seldom heard in the body, to speak of the regrets he feels for previous policy in respect to so meritorious a measure; and goes on to portray the claims of the old soldiers on the Government, and reproducing his Christmas Dream, attunes his voice to the memories of the anthems and the hymns of freedom, until the Senators flock in to listen, and the buzz is awed, and even the clock ticks more quietly, and the pages imitate Darby Dilks in his statuesque repose by the marble column.

The Committee rises. More jargon at the desk. Speaker and Chairman bow and cross-bow, and advance and retire and cross-fire, and the chant announces more audibly than it has ever before sung that in the Bill entitled, etc., the House concur, and it will be sent to the President for approval.

A hush, and then a buzz, and then a shrill " Hurrah!" from the gallery. It is the veteran on his feet—Ned and Agnes vainly pulling at his elbows. " Hurrah for Washington and Jackson!" rings the shrill cry. Bustle—bustle —by the door and in the aisles. All eyes up-stairs, and groups clustering by the pillar opposite the Ladies' Gallery.

" It is one of the veterans himself!" exclaimed Darby, on recognizing Captain Sherburne ; but almost ready the next moment to bite his tongue out, as he sees the pages exult before him.

" Have him out! have him down!" calls some of the lobby ; and members beckon deprecatingly to the gallery door-keeper, who is officiously interrupting the most striking tableau these benches have seen for many a day. More bustle—and the tableau breaks up. The door-keeper has left his place by the stair-head, and trills of barks resound through the House, now entirely thrown off its equilibrium.

" Bow-wow-wow!" roars Ranger, no longer awed by the fat door-keeper, but leaping up into the old man's arms as he is held by the door-keeper, and then bolting at that fat functionary's legs as he smells out the trouble.

" Move we adjourn!" is heard above the bow-wow, buzz, and bustle ; and amidst the chant a gavel falls, and·a rush is made for the outer chamber, where the old man already is, with Ned crazy with laughter, and Agnes half-dead with confusion and fear, the dog still yelping like mad, and the lobby crowd killing the buzz outright in emulating the old man's shrill and repeated hurrahs for Washington and Jackson !

VI.

WHILE ten thousand urchins and damsels over all the land were exclaiming, in holiday chorus, "What a pity New-Year's Day should come on Sunday!" a party of four at the side door of St. Bridget's were congratulating each other because New-Year's Day and Sunday did meet together. There was the Congressman and the Captain— he had found his member at last—and Ned and Agnes also. The snow, seldom seen in the Federal metropolis, had fallen liberally overnight, and Ned, commissioned for an early carriage, had secured almost the only hack-sleigh in town. Joyfully the sleigh-bells pealed at the door of Darby Dilks, while the household were at breakfast; for there came uncle and nephew to redeem the promise of the church meeting. Lightly beat the hearts of all, and lightly flew the heels of the exhilarated horses to the church door.

"Valley Forge," said the uncle, pointing from the avenue over the snowy landscape far away, as they drove along.

"Lexington rather," answered the old man, sadly pointing to a company of soldiers drawn up on the square preparing for a comrade's funeral.

"But never the prison-ship, or suffering, or worriment any more," added the Congressman, taking the hands of the Captain, while tears streamed down the cheeks of all.

"Are we not very late?" asked Agnes, suddenly, as the clock chimed its quarter.

"Yes, late for what you were expecting to do," said Mr. Lillington, gallantly taking her hand and handing her from the sleigh.

Before she could ask his meaning, he aided to lift the veteran carefully to the icy walk.

"Ned, you shall take Captain Sherburne, and I will escort Miss Montrose."

"Call me Agnes, if you please;" and she flushed as she said it.

"Not yet. Miss Montrose to-day; but Miss Montrose no longer than to-day."

"The church service is over," said Ned, looking through the door.

"I knew we were late," said she; "and oh, how we had counted on this service!"

The uncle smiled, and, taking her arm still more closely in his own, drew her into the little robing-room where stood the parish priest.

"I have a little favor to ask," said he, who held the trembling arm. "It is your grandfather's birthday, and the first day of the year. How better can we celebrate both than by one present all around? No need of gaud and show—that would ill become you—I have a special dispensation from the bishop, or rather our good friend there holds it, who also has taken to your convent the benefaction for supporting many Sister Agneses in your place. Present to Ned a wife, and to me a daughter—not a niece—for you are doubly—"

He paused, and before his agitation and kindness maidenly reserve fled, and only girlish trustfulness remained.

She placed her hand in his and smiled. Who was it at that instant rushed forward, and, lightly brushing bonnet-strings and furs and mantle, left her ready for the veil and altar? who but Ned?

The priest smiled, and, motioning to the side-door, they all entered—the fast-expiring name of Montrose breathing gently on the lips of bride and groom and kinsman—the younger supporting the oldest, and the oldest lover and the newest beloved arm in arm. And so before the altar.

The old hero, waiting not for word or sign, nor caring whether it were etiquette or not, knelt down before the rail, and there continued, never looking up during the long service which followed. Agnes seemed almost a bride of the Church as the canonical veil was folded around her form. Ned's heart beat high with holy joy, and amidst the clouds of incense floating around the altar, the uncle heard the singing voices and saw the salient features of his Christmas Dream.

*　　*　　*　　*　　*　　*　　*　　*　　*　　*

"And now, my dear Sir, wishing you a Happy New Year, and congratulating you upon attaining your ninetieth birthday," said Mr. Lillington to Captain Sherburne, as several hours afterward they were gathered together at the New-Year's dinner-table—"Ned and I having had a sudden New-Year's present, nothing remains but for your grandchild, Mrs. Leslie, here to bestow her present and your reward."

Rising from her seat, and blushing as she heard her new appellation, Agnes kissed the beloved forehead, while the scar broadened and reddened with delight. Then taking from beneath her plate a fold of paper in a long envelope, she said : " And this, grandfather, is the certified copy of your Act of Congress—a New-Year's present—not only for yourself, but for many more old comrades besides, to whom tardy justice arrives through your endeavors."

" Bravo—bravo, indeed ! " cried her uncle ; " Henry Clay himself could not have said that better."

" And allow me also to show you, Sir, the original Act, that is loaned to me by permission of the State Department, with the signature of the President himself— Andrew Jackson—firm and bold, as one hero's autograph should be that consecrates an act of justice to so many other heroes ;" and the old man put the writing to his lips. " But a truce to sadness," he added, as the tears began to flow upon the furrowed cheek ; "you are a lobby member no ,longer, and therefore you shall have your hunger appeased before the end of the feast. After that we will discuss Ned's future and your own ; for we hope to share many Christmases and New Years together from this day forward."

Returning to the table, the old man dropped his envelope, and Ranger, darting from his place of privilege under the table, seized it in his mouth caressingly and sported with it round the room. This incident restored the humor and hilarity of all; and while the butler is adroitly occupied in extricating the Bill from the last jaws of danger that will ever surround it, let us hasten to drop the curtain over " THE CONGRESSMAN'S CHRISTMAS DREAM AND THE LOBBY-MEMBER'S HAPPY NEW YEAR."

www.ingramcontent.com/pod-product-compliance
Lightning Source LLC
Chambersburg PA
CBHW032153010726
47493CB00008BA/2683

*9 7 8 3 3 3 7 2 9 2 0 5 8 *